A MESSAGE TO PARENTS

Reading good books to young children is a crucial factor in a child's psychological and intellectual development. It promotes a mutually warm and satisfying relationship between parent and child and enhances the child's awareness of the world around him. It stimulates the child's imagination and lays a foundation for the development of the skills necessary to support the critical thinking process. In addition, the parent who reads to his child helps him to build vocabulary and other prerequisite skills for the child's own successful reading.

In order to provide parents and children with books which will do these things, Brown Watson has published this series of small books specially designed for young children. These books are factual, fanciful, humourous, questioning and adventurous. A library acquired in this inexpensive way will provide many hours of pleasurable and profitable reading for parents and children.

Sleeping Beauty

Text by Maureen Spurgeon

Brown Watson

© 1990 Brown Watson (Leicester) Ltd.
ENGLAND.
Startright Elf and their respective logos
are trademarks of Macmillan Inc.
Printed and bound in the German Democratic Republic.

THERE was once a king and queen who seemed to have everything that anyone could possibly want. They had a lovely palace, huge estates, and all the people in the kingdom loved them. Yet, still they longed for just one thing more — a child of their own.

Then, after many a sad and lonely year, a baby daughter was born.

The king and queen were so happy.

"We shall give a party to celebrate," announced the king.

"And all the fairies shall be invited!" cried the queen.

So the invitations were written, ready for birds to take them to all parts of the kingdom. Nobody saw one invitation fluttering down into the lake . . .

It was the invitation for the Fairy Carabos.

When she heard there was to be a royal party, and she was not invited, she was furious!

She ran to the palace, where the other fairies were gathered around the cradle, ready to bless the royal baby with gifts of kindness, happiness and beauty.

"Hah!" screamed a cruel, mocking voice. "Heed the spell of Carabos! On her fifteenth birthday, the princess will prick her finger on a spindle, and die!"

With a wild cackle of laughter which rang all round the palace, Carabos swept out, nodding her head in satisfaction to hear the gasps of horror behind her.

The fairies knew Carabos was far more powerful than them.

"But, perhaps," one said at last, "we can put our magic together and change the spell, just a little ..."

"It means the princess will sleep for a hundred years when she pricks her finger," she told the king and queen. "But at least she will not die."

"All the spindles in the kingdom must be broken!" cried the king. "Then our child will be safe!"

Soon, the evil spell was forgotten. The princess grew beautiful, often dreaming of the handsome prince she hoped to marry, one day.

As the day of her fifteenth birthday approached, the king and queen planned the most splendid party. All the servants were very busy.

So the princess was left alone to wander through the grounds by herself. And that is how she came across a little door she had never seen before . . .

Soon, the princess was climbing a staircase which led to the very top of a high tower. There sat an old woman at a spinning wheel — something completely new to her...

"Come, learn to spin, my dear," cackled the old woman. "Just take the spindle . . ."

And in one terrible instant, the wicked spell of Carabos came true!

The beautiful young princess pricked her finger and fell to the ground. And even the wild screams of laughter from Carabos faded into complete silence.

Throughout the kingdom, nothing moved. The grass, the bushes and hedges around the palace grew tall and thick.

The story of the Sleeping Beauty became a legend, a tale which parents told their children. Until, one day, a brave prince decided to try and discover the truth . . .

On and on he rode, until he came to the forest, so thick and dark, there seemed no way in. But, as he raised his sword to cut through the greenery, a strange thing happened . . .

The forest of trees and bushes parted, so that he could lead his horse to the palace! Nothing had changed since the day when the evil spell of Carabos had come true...

The prince went through the little door and climbed the stairs. The last thing he expected to see was the princess, still young, still fast asleep . . .

She was so lovely, the prince fell in love with her at once. As he bent to kiss her, she opened her eyes and gave him a sweet smile.

At the same moment, the birds outside the window began singing, the leaves rustled in the breeze, and a bell sounded in the kitchen. The long sleep was over!